W9-BOO-505

•Barrow

Beaufort Sea

Arctic National
Wildlife Refuge

Yukon River

ASKA   •Fairbanks

CANADA

Denali National Park

Iditarod Trail

Matanuska River Valley

Prince William Sound

Anchorage

Kenai River

Glacier Bay   Chilkat Bald Eagle Preserve
⭐ Juneau

Tongass National   Admiralty Island
Forest

Gulf of Alaska

◉	Site visited by the eagle
★	State capital
●	City
⎯⎯	River
⎯⎯	Iditarod Trail
- - -	Alternate Iditarod route

BIG Alaska

Journey Across America's Most Amazing State

Debbie S. Miller   Illustrations by Jon Van Zyle

Walker & Company New York

Dear Everett,

Thanks for coming to visit me in Fairbanks, Alaska. I'm so glad you got to see the biggest mountain in North America, the Tongass National Forest, and other beautiful places in our state. Thanks especially for inspiring me to write this book about a wild bald eagle and his journey across Alaska. Come visit me anytime!

Sincerely,

Debbie S. Miller

For Everett, the wandering eagle, who visited me in Alaska, and for all the students at Central Elementary School in Wilmette, Illinois —D.S.M.

For Walter, the father I never had, from the son you never had; and for Maida, my other caring mother —J.V.Z.

Text copyright © 2006 by Debbie S. Miller
Illustrations copyright © 2006 by Jon Van Zyle

First published in the United States of America in 2006 by Walker Publishing Company, Inc. Distributed to the trade by Holtzbrinck Publishers

For information about permission to reproduce selections from this book, write to Permissions, Walker & Company, 104 Fifth Avenue, New York, New York 10011.

Library of Congress Cataloging-in-Publication Data

Miller, Debbie S.
  Big Alaska / Debbie S. Miller ; illustrations by Jon Van Zyle.
    p. cm.
  Includes bibliographical references and index.
  ISBN-10: 0-8027-8069-5 (hardcover : alk. paper)
  ISBN-13: 978-0-8027-8069-0 (hardcover : alk. paper)
  ISBN-10: 0-8027-8070-9 (reinforced : alk. paper)
  ISBN-13: 978-0-8027-8070-6 (reinforced : alk. paper)
  1. Alaska—Description and travel—Juvenile literature. I. Van Zyle, Jon, ill. II. Title.
  F910.5.M55 2006
  917.98—dc22
                                        2005024086

The artist used acrylic on untempered Masonite panels to create the illustrations for this book.

Book design by Nicole Gastonguay

Visit Walker & Company's Web site at www.walkeryoungreaders.com

Printed in China

10 9 8 7 6 5 4 3 2 1

Many thanks to all of the federal and state biologists and educators who answered questions about Alaska's parks, wildlife refuges, and forests that are featured in this book. A special thanks to Jim Tingey and his fourth grade class for sending Everett to Alaska and guiding this project. Thanks to Richard Nelson for showing Everett Southeast Alaska, Nancy Ferrell for her help and love of nonfiction, Kathy Benner at the Juneau Raptor Center, and to Brian McCaffery for his assistance.

INTRODUCTION

Alaska is a vast land of natural wonders, magnificent beauty, and extraordinary wilderness. America's largest state holds the biggest mountains and temperate rain forest in North America, along with the world's largest bears, moose, and salmon. Alaska has millions of lakes and wild rivers, stunning parks and wildlife refuges, and one of the longest chains of islands in the world. The name Alaska comes from the Aleut word *Alyeska* (Ally-ES-ka), which means "the great land."

Yes, Alaska is BIG! If you place Alaska on the continental United States, it would stretch from the Pacific to the Atlantic coasts, and from northern Minnesota to Georgia. Alaska is more than twice as big as Texas, yet it is one of the most sparsely populated states. With about 650,000 people, there are nearly twice as many caribou as there are humans.

Alaska is so great that its scale is unlike any place else on earth. The state is bordered by 2 oceans and 3 seas. If you include the shores of all the islands, Alaska has 33,900 miles of coastline, which is farther than the circumference of the earth if you walked along the equator. In Alaska you can walk in a rain forest, climb glaciated peaks, or hike across the treeless tundra in the Arctic.

America's national emblem, the majestic bald eagle, inhabits many areas of Alaska. Through the eyes of a bald eagle, this story will take you on a journey across The Great Land. Come fly with this eagle and see some of Alaska's biggest and most extraordinary features. . . .

ADMIRALTY ISLAND
Largest Concentration of Bald Eagle Nests

Feathered legs outstretched, the bald eagle glides above the quiet cove. *SPLASH!* Alaska's largest bird of prey cuts through the water and snatches a red salmon. He flies along the Inside Passage toward his birthplace on Admiralty Island. This densely wooded island has the largest concentration of nesting bald eagles in the world.

TONGASS NATIONAL FOREST
Largest Temperate Rain Forest

The old-growth forest on Admiralty Island is part of the
biggest temperate rain forest on earth, the Tongass
National Forest. This forest of spruce and hemlock
covers much of Alaska's southeast region, known as the
Panhandle.

The eagle perches on the limb of a giant Sitka
spruce, the largest tree within the rain forest. These
majestic trees thrive in this foggy area, where it can rain
more than 100 inches per year. While eagles, marbled
murrelets, and woodpeckers nest in the spruce, deer and
bears browse on the forest floor beneath the dense tangle
of lush branches.

GLACIER BAY NATIONAL PARK
Highest Coastal Mountains

Wandering up Alaska's coast, the eagle skirts Juneau, the state capital. Wedged between mountains and sea, this isolated capital can be reached only by airplane or boat. The eagle pumps his broad wings above green islands, steep mountains, and ribbons of water that cascade into the sea.

He flies toward the ice-bound St. Elias Mountains, the highest coastal mountains in the world. Enormous glaciers wrap around the mountain ridges and peaks, flowing into one another. These huge rivers of ice spill into Glacier Bay.

THRRRUMP!!! A thunderous roar booms across the water. A towering skyscraper of ice is crashing into the bay. The calving of this tidewater glacier causes small invertebrates to rise to the surface, and hundreds of black-legged kittiwakes begin feasting on them.

PRINCE WILLIAM SOUND
Worst Oil Spill

The eagle follows America's longest coastline, mile after mile of empty, wild beaches. At Prince William Sound, playful sea otters float on their backs and the shiny dorsal fins of orcas rise and fall. Suddenly, a humpback whale hurls its massive body out of the water.

The eagle soars above the port of Valdez and the Trans-Alaska Pipeline. In addition to holding marine life, Prince William Sound is also the site of the worst oil spill in U.S. history. In 1989, hundreds of thousands of animals died from this devastating tanker spill. The Sound is recovering from this tragic accident.

Above the Sound, the eagle climbs toward Thompson Pass. This high pass once received the biggest annual snowfall in Alaska's history, more than 81 feet of snow! During the winter, Valdez gets the most snow of any Alaska community—an average of 25 feet per year.

MATANUSKA RIVER VALLEY
Heaviest Vegetables on Earth

The eagle continues his northwest journey across the Chugach Mountains. He discovers a broad, fertile valley that is cradled between the snow-capped peaks.

The valley is a patchwork of farms, gardens, hay fields, and clusters of homes and buildings. This is the Matanuska River Valley near Palmer, the most productive agricultural area in Alaska.

With 24-hour summer light and rich soil, some of the heaviest vegetables on earth have grown here. Imagine a 105-pound cabbage, an 18-pound carrot, and a 63-pound head of celery!

ANCHORAGE
Strongest North American Earthquake

Beyond the Matanuska Valley, the eagle follows Knik Arm, a huge estuary that flows into Cook Inlet. In the distance are tall buildings, ships in a harbor, and a graceful mountain known as the Sleeping Lady. He is approaching Alaska's largest city, Anchorage.

Above the busy streets and quiet parks, it is difficult to imagine that one of the most powerful earthquakes in the world devastated this city in 1964. This violent quake, measuring 9.2 on the Richter scale, is the second-largest earthquake ever recorded. More than 100 people died in the tsunami that followed the earthquake. Tsunami waves damaged Alaska's coastal towns such as Valdez and Kodiak, and communities as far away as Crescent City in California.

KENAI RIVER

Biggest King Salmon

Traveling south, the eagle explores the Kenai River. The biggest king salmon in the world have been caught in this river—weighing nearly 100 pounds!

While the eagle waits for opportunities to scavenge, a fisherman struggles to land a huge king salmon. The giant king is nearly as tall as the fisherman.

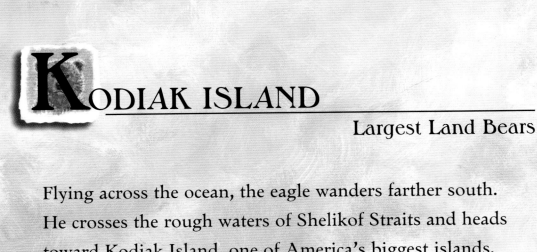

KODIAK ISLAND

Largest Land Bears

Flying across the ocean, the eagle wanders farther south. He crosses the rough waters of Shelikof Straits and heads toward Kodiak Island, one of America's biggest islands.

A blustery, fog-shrouded land greets the eagle. He seeks shelter from the strong gales in a forest. Beneath his perch, a Kodiak brown bear and her cubs lumber into the valley. Kodiak bears are the biggest land bears in the world. This bear family is heading toward their favorite fishing stream.

KATMAI NATIONAL PARK

Most Active Volcanoes

Beyond Kodiak Island, the eagle wings his way along the Alaska Peninsula toward the long chain of Aleutian Islands that arc westward. Seabird colonies speckle the rocky cliffs, and alpine tundra graces the snow-covered volcanoes.

Alaska has approximately 50 active volcanoes, more than all other states combined. Circling around Mount Katmai, the eagle soars above the site of the 20th century's

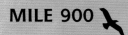

biggest eruption. In 1912, the Katmai eruption lasted for more than 2 days. The deafening blast could be heard for several hundred miles. The skies grew dark and ash piled up 700 feet deep, turning a lush valley into a moonscape.

The eagle now flies above that same valley, the Valley of 10,000 Smokes. This barren land of hardened ash, known as tuff, surrounds more than a dozen active volcanoes.

WALRUS ISLANDS SANCTUARY
Largest Gathering of Walruses

The eagle turns northwest, crossing Bristol Bay, a rich body of water that holds the greatest abundance of sockeye salmon. While he swoops down for a meal, thousands of walruses bask in the sunshine on the shores of Round Island. Each summer, male walruses haul themselves out on this island's rocky beaches. Some of these bulls weigh nearly two tons. Lying on top of each other, the huge bulls pack together like a big pile of puppies.

The Walrus Islands of Bristol Bay offer a safe resting habitat for the largest concentration of walruses in North America.

YUKON KUSKOQUIM DELTA
Biggest North American River Delta

Beyond Bristol Bay, the eagle approaches the biggest river delta in North America. The mighty Yukon and Kuskoquim rivers and their tributaries form these vast wetlands. Flat, marshy tundra stretches out for hundreds of miles. This pond-specked land is home to millions of ground-nesting shorebirds and waterfowl.

Cla-ha, cla-ha, cla-ha, an emperor goose calls. Alarmed by a stalking arctic fox, the goose raises her wings, ready to protect the nest. From above, the eagle catches a distant glimpse of the goose defending her eggs.

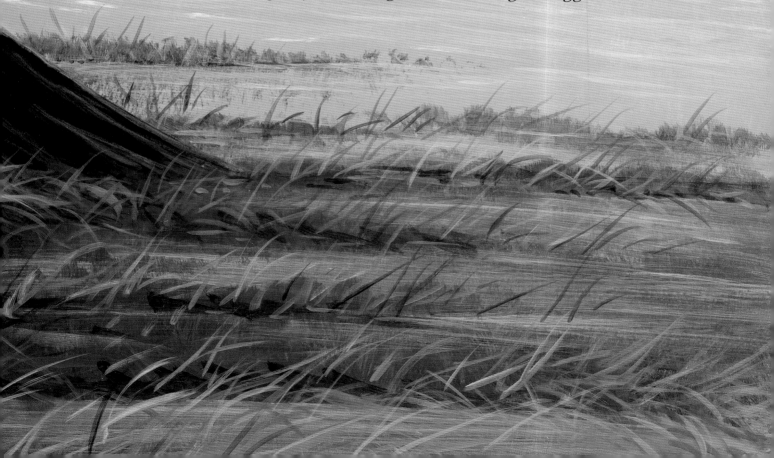

YUKON RIVER AND TRIBUTARIES
Biggest Gold Rush

Flying farther north, the eagle follows the curving Yukon
River across Interior Alaska. Small villages hug the banks
of the river, and people are checking their fishwheels for
salmon.

In the late 1800s, prospectors discovered gold along the Yukon and its tributaries. The 1896 Klondike strike sparked the world's biggest gold rush. Tens of thousands of miners stampeded into the Yukon Territory and Alaska. Communities such as Dawson, Fairbanks, Circle City, and Ruby grew around the mining camps. Today, Alaska continues to be one of the top gold-producing states.

ARCTIC NATIONAL WILDLIFE REFUGE

America's Largest Wildlife Refuge

Gradually the forest grows less dense, and the spruce trees look spindly. The eagle has reached the *taiga*, a Russian word meaning "the land of little sticks." Above the Arctic Circle, the winters are long, and the ground beneath the soft carpet of tundra is permanently frozen.

Grunt, snort, click. Grunt, snort, click. With hooves clicking, thousands of caribou are migrating through the

Brooks Range, majestic mountains that sweep across
northern Alaska. The eagle lands on a pinnacle and
watches the amazing procession across the arctic tundra.
He has reached America's biggest wildlife refuge, the
Arctic National Wildlife Refuge. This wild corner of
Alaska is home to a rich diversity of life, including polar
bears, muskoxen, snowy owls, and wolves.

DENALI NATIONAL PARK
Tallest North American Mountain

An arctic storm brings gale-force winds and snow into the
Brooks Range. The harsh autumn weather drives the eagle
south to find a sheltered habitat. He flies over the forest,
along winding rivers framed by golden trees. Sandhill
cranes, geese, and swans are beginning their southern
migrations along the Tanana River near Fairbanks.

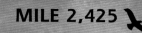

The weather clears and fresh snow dusts the tallest mountain in North America, Mount McKinley. This magnificent mountain is also known as Denali, an Athabaskan word meaning "the high one." In Denali National Park, the eagle spots a pack of wolves that are hunting in the valley.

 IDITAROD TRAIL
Longest Sled Dog Race

October days grow short and cool, and wet snow plasters
every branch and twig in the forest. The eagle senses that he
must keep moving south. He flies on through the towering
mountains of the Alaska Range toward the distant coast.

Tucked in the forest, the eagle spots some cabins with
yards full of sled dogs. He roosts in a nearby spruce tree

and watches a dog musher drive his team of huskies down the historic Iditarod Trail. The team is training for the 1,150-mile race to Nome that will begin in March. As the dogs race by, beautiful curtains of northern lights dance across the evening sky.

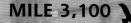

Chilkat Bald Eagle Preserve
Largest Gathering of Eagles

The eagle soars on, returning to southeast Alaska, near his birthplace. From his memory, the eagle knows that now is the season when thousands of eagles gather at a special place in the Chilkat River Valley.

Along this salmon-rich river, cottonwood trees are specked with the white heads of bald eagles. The Chilkat River Valley is an important feeding site for the largest concentration of bald eagles in the world.

The bald eagle joins other eagles that are feasting on the spawning chum salmon. As big snowflakes float through the cold sky, the eagle is no longer alone. In a few months, he will pair up with his first mate. Together they will build a huge nest near the top of an old Sitka spruce tree, where this eagle's journey first began.

Alaska FACTS

Alaska: The state's name comes from the Aleut word *Alyeska*, which means "the great land."

Land Area: 570,374 square miles, or 365 million acres. Alaska is the largest state in the United States, 2½ times bigger than Texas.

Coastline: Alaska's shoreline is twice the length of all other coastal states combined. Including islands, Alaska has 33,900 miles of coastline.

National Parks, Wildlife Refuges, and Forests: Most of our nation's protected conservation areas are located in Alaska. Alaska has 15 national parks and preserves, 16 wildlife refuges, and 2 national forests, which comprise 40% of the state.

Population: Approximately 650,000. Alaska is a vast state of wilderness with relatively few people. The city of Chicago has nearly 3 million people, more than 4 times the total number of people in Alaska.

Native People: Most of Alaska's Native people are Eskimo, Indian, and Aleut. Many live in scattered villages with distinct cultural traditions and languages. More than 100,000 Native people, in 8 regional groups, live in Alaska.

Russian Purchase: In 1867, the United States purchased Alaska from Russia for $7.2 million, about 2¢ an acre. Secretary of State William Seward negotiated the sale. Many referred to the purchase as "Seward's folly" because people thought Alaska was a frozen, worthless wasteland.

Statehood: Alaska became America's 49th state on January 3, 1959.

Capital: Juneau. This isolated community is Alaska's third-largest city. It is the only state capital in the U.S. that is not accessible by road. You must travel by boat or plane to reach this beautiful city wedged between mountains and sea.

Farthest North City: Barrow. The Inupiat Eskimo community of Barrow is located 350 miles above the Arctic Circle. About 4,500 people live in this remote town on the shores of the Arctic Ocean.

Economy: Oil and gas development is Alaska's biggest industry. Oil revenues fund about 80% of Alaska's government services. Tourism is also a major industry, employing many Alaskans. Fisheries, mining, and forest products are other important sectors of the economy.

State
SYMBOLS

Motto: North to the Future

Nickname: The Last Frontier

Bird: willow ptarmigan

Flower: forget-me-not

Insect: four-spot skimmer dragonfly

Fish: king salmon

Fossil: woolly mammoth

Gem: jade

Land mammal: moose

Marine mammal: bowhead whale

Mineral: gold

Sport: dog mushing

Tree: Sitka spruce

Flag: The Alaska state flag was designed in 1926 by Benny Benson, a young seventh-grade Aleut boy. Benson entered his design in a territorial flag contest. The flag consists of eight gold stars representing the Big Dipper and North Star on a midnight-blue sky.

Climate
RECORDS

Land of Extremes

Highest temperature:
100° F, at Fort Yukon, June 27, 1915

Lowest temperature:
-80° F, at Prospect Creek, January 23, 1971

Most snowfall:
974.5" at Thompson Pass, 1952–53

Least snowfall:
3" at Barrow, 1935–36

Highest recorded wind speed:
143 mph at Dutch Harbor, November, 2000

Alaska's SPECIAL PLACES

Admiralty Island: This lush island supports the largest concentration of bald eagle nests in the world. One study found 1,029 nests on Admiralty Island, about 1 nest per mile of coastline. Most bald eagles nest near saltwater in large Sitka spruce trees more than 400 years old. A pair of eagles may use and enlarge the same nest year after year. Some of these huge nests can weigh as much as a small truck after many years of use. Visit www.fs.fed.us/r10/tongass/districts/admiralty.

Tongass National Forest: Most of Southeast Alaska, including Admiralty Island, is part of the largest national forest in America, the 17-million acre Tongass National Forest. Alaska's state tree, the Sitka spruce, dominates this temperate coastal rain forest. The Sitka spruce is the largest of all spruce trees. These magnificent trees can reach 250 feet in height, and 5 to 10 feet in diameter. They may live for 500 to 850 years. Visit www.fs.fed.us/r10/tongass.

Glacier Bay National Park: Alaska has approximately 100,000 glaciers, more than all other states combined. Scenic Glacier Bay is surrounded by the St. Elias Mountains, rising to over 15,000 feet. Nine tidewater glaciers flow down from these mountains, spilling into the saltwater. Towering blocks of ice, up to 200 feet high, can break loose and crash into the bay. Huge icebergs may float in the bay for a week or more, providing perches for eagles and cormorants and safe resting sites for harbor seals. Visit www.nps.gov/glba.

Prince William Sound: This is a marine haven for humpback whales, sea otters, Steller sea lions, harbor seals, Dall porpoise, and orcas. In March 1989, the Exxon Valdez oil tanker struck Bligh Reef and spilled more than 11 million gallons of crude oil into Prince William Sound. Hundreds of thousands of birds perished and thousands of marine mammals died. During the clean up, as many as 11,000 people worked to remove the toxic oil. Today, scientists continue to monitor the sound, which is in the process of recovering. To learn more about the oil spill and the recovery of Prince William Sound, visit http://response.restoration.noaa.gov/kids/spills.html.

Matanuska River Valley: This valley is the most productive agricultural area in Alaska. Every year local farmers produce large vegetables in its fertile soil. With 24-hour light, plants grow quickly in June and July. Many national- and world-record vegetables have been grown and exhibited at the annual Alaska State Fair. To see some of these giant vegetables visit www.alaskagiant.com.

Anchorage: Nearly half of Alaska's population lives in Anchorage, the state's largest city. The 1964 earthquake caused extensive damage to the city. Its main business street, 4th Avenue, dropped 20–30 feet down into the earth. More than 300 homes and buildings were totally destroyed. Of the 131 people that died, 119 deaths were caused by the tsunami that damaged coastal communities such as Kodiak and Valdez. To learn more about earthquakes in Alaska visit www.aeic.alaska.edu/seis.

Kenai River: Four species of salmon are found in this popular fishing river. In 1985, the largest king salmon (chinook) was caught by a fisherman in the Kenai River. The record-setting fish weighed 97 pounds, 4 oz. In addition to fish, the Kenai Peninsula is home to an abundance of moose, brown and black bears, caribou, Dall sheep, trumpeter swans, and other waterfowl. To learn more about this region visit the Kenai National Wildlife Refuge at http://kenai.fws.gov.

Kodiak Island: Known for its enormous Kodiak brown bears, this is the second-largest island in America. About 2,500 bears live on this island, thriving on some of the 25 million salmon that use the streams and rivers for spawning. With such a rich diet, these huge bears can weigh as much as 1,500 pounds, the largest land omnivores in the world. When fish are not available, the bears graze on berries, grasses, and other plants. Visit the Kodiak National Wildlife Refuge Web site at http://kodiak.fws.gov.

Katmai National Park: The 1912 Katmai eruption was the largest volcanic eruption ever recorded in North America—50 times bigger than the 1980 eruption of Mount St. Helens. Volcanic ash and dust darkened the sky for more than 2 days and world temperatures were affected for several years. With 15 active volcanoes, Katmai National Park is one of the most active volcanic centers in the world. The volcanoes are part of the Pacific Ring of Fire. To learn more about Alaska's volcanoes visit www.avo.alaska.edu. To learn more about Katmai National Park visit www.nps.gov/katm.

Walrus Islands Sanctuary: Seven craggy islands in Bristol Bay are part of the Walrus Islands State Game Sanctuary. Round Island is world famous as a major haul-out site for huge concentrations of male walruses. As the northern pack ice recedes in the spring, the walruses return to the islands to haul out and rest. As many as 14,000 walruses have been counted in 1 day on Round Island. The walruses migrate northward in the fall, when the sea ice advances. To learn about this sanctuary visit http://www.wildlife.alaska.gov.

Yukon Kuskoquim Delta: The Yukon and Kuskoquim rivers and their tributaries form the largest delta in North America. Each spring millions of birds migrate to the delta region from every state and province in North America. To learn more about the importance of these wetlands, visit the Yukon Delta National Wildlife Refuge Web site at http://yukondelta.fws.gov.

Yukon River: The word Yukon means "big river" in Athabaskan. In the U.S. the Yukon ranks 3rd in length after the Mississippi and the Missouri rivers. Numerous Athabaskan Indian and Yup'ik Eskimo villages are located along this 2,300-mile waterway that extends into Canada's Yukon territory. The historic Yukon was the main transportation route during the Klondike Gold Rush. Tens of thousands of prospectors explored the Yukon drainage. To learn more about the Klondike gold rush visit www.nps.gov/klgo.

Arctic National Wildlife Refuge: The Arctic Refuge has one of the greatest diversities of arctic animals on earth. About the size of South Carolina, America's biggest wildlife refuge is home to shaggy muskoxen, wolves, grizzly bears, polar bears, and one of the largest caribou herds in North America. Birds from 6 continents and every U.S. state migrate to the Arctic Refuge to nest and raise their young. Oil and gas development has been proposed on the coastal plain of the Arctic Refuge. This controversial area is a sensitive birthplace for many species such as caribou, muskoxen, and polar bears. Visit http://arctic.fws.gov.

Denali National Park: Each year more than 1,000 people try to climb Mt. McKinley, the highest mountain in North America. Less than half of the climbers reach the summit of this 20,320-foot mountain, also known as Denali. Subzero temperatures, thin air, and winds upward of 100 miles per hour present dangerous challenges. The youngest person to climb Denali was Galen Johnson, an 11-year-old boy from Talkeetna, Alaska. To find out more about the park's abundant wildlife and spectacular mountain scenery visit www.nps.gov/dena.

Iditarod Trail: The 1,150 mile Iditarod Trail Sled Dog Race is the longest dog race in the world. Since 1973, mushers have competed in this March race from Anchorage to Nome. The fastest time on record is that of musher Martin Buser. In 2002, he finished the race in 8 days, 22 hours, and 46 minutes. In 1925, 20 dog mushers raced to Nome in a team relay to save the town from a possible diphtheria epidemic. The Iditarod Sled Dog Race commemorates the heroic efforts of these mushers and dogs. To learn more about the Iditarod Race visit www.iditarod.com.

Chilkat Bald Eagle Preserve: This preserve protects the world's largest concentration of bald eagles and their critical salmon-rich river habitat. During the fall and winter, a large reservoir of open water on the Chilkat River provides ideal feeding conditions for the hungry eagles. Five species of salmon spawn in the Chilkat and its tributaries. More than 3,000 eagles have been counted within the preserve between October and February. To learn more about the Chilkat Bald Eagle Preserve and other state parks visit www.dnr.state.ak.us/parks/units.

ARCTIC OCEAN

Chukchi Sea

• Nome

Yukon River ⬤

Kuskoquim River

Yukon Kuskoquim Delta ⬤

Walrus Islands
State Game Sanctuary ⬤

Katmai National Park ⬤

Bering Sea

Kodiak Island ⬤

PACIFIC OCEAN